1000

Sweets
& Treats

Have fun completing the
sticker and doodling activities!
Pull out the sticker sheets and keep
them by you when you complete
each page. There are also extra
stickers to use throughout this
book or anywhere you want!

make
believe
ideas

Busy bake sale!

Sticker tasty toppings!

Decorate the baked treats.

2

4

Jelly beans

Candy circles

Color amazing treats!

Rocket bar

Rocket bar

Rocket bar

Use the grid to copy the chocolate.

6

Find the missing stickers.

Cookie race!

Follow the lines to see who gets which fruit.

Bake a brilliant pie!

8

Sticker fruit fillings in the pie.

Color the cherry muffins.

Sticker and color chocolate on the fruit.

9

Dipped-fruit fun!

Doodle funny faces on the fruit!

Finish a cool candy gallery!

How many candies can you color in this picture?

Pumpkin party!

Use your stickers
to create fun faces.

Sticker m
crown!

13

Color the giant pumpkin orange!

Find the missing stickers, then circle the one that is different.

Finish the pumpkin lollipops.

Make tasty orange snacks!

Decorate the treats with color and stickers.

Draw fun faces on the candies!

FILL the snack bowls!

Toffee treats!

Cheesy bites!

How many pumpkin cookies can you count?

Create cute costumes!

Use color and stickers to finish the costumes.

Finish the tasty top hat.

Rabbit has dropped all the candies. Help him find them!

Hop! Hop!

Roar!

17

Roar!

Sticker spots on Dinosaur's tail!

Color Dino's big feet!

Decorate the candy-cane glasses.

Sticker pumpkins on the T-shirt!

18

It's party time!

Find the missing stickers to prepare the perfect party!

19

Find the missing apples.

Feed the hungry pumpkin with lots of treats.

Yum!

Yum!

Build a birthday cake!

Color the party hats!

20

22

What is lost in the swirly cream?

Find the missing stickers.

Candy designer!
Create your own candy.

Cool costumes!

Finish the accessories!

Add candy to the hat.

Finish the banana swo

Color and sticker more candy!

Decorate the dog's candy kennel!

Woof!

Fruit fiesta!

Use your stickers to finish the fruit pattern.

Color and sticker the fruity yogurt pots!

27

Sundae surprise!

Sticker toppings!

Find two fudge chunks!

Find the missing stickers.

29

Add color.

Create a monster cake!

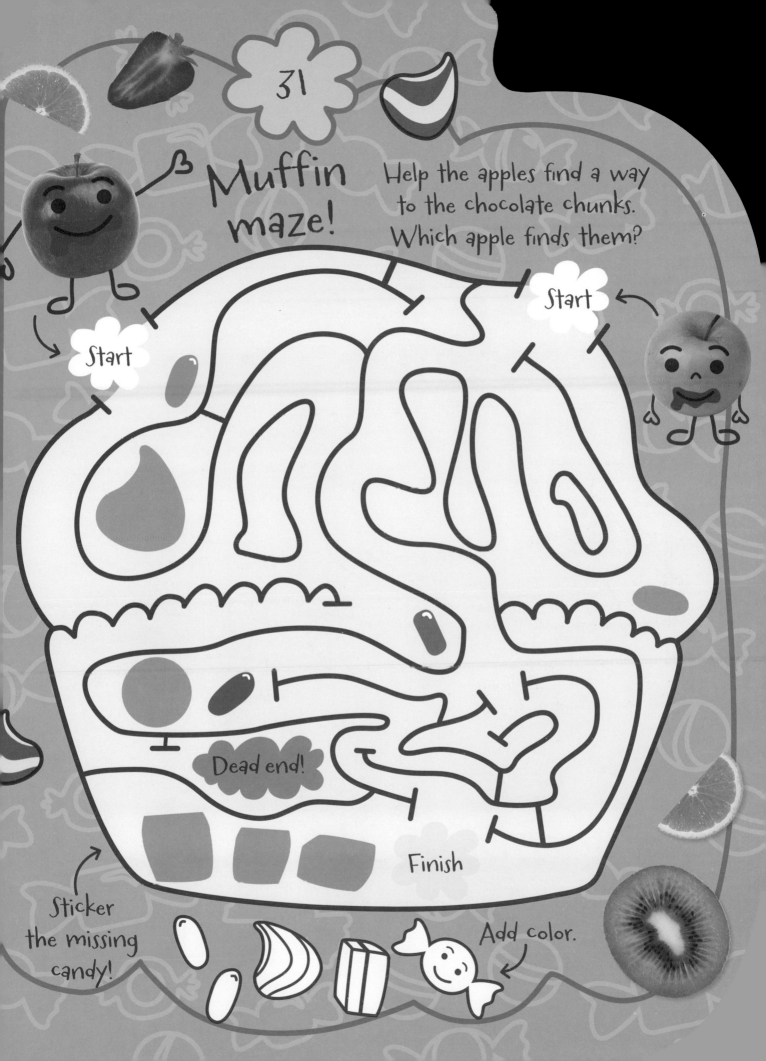

Muffin maze!

Help the apples find a way to the chocolate chunks. Which apple finds them?

Start

Start

Dead end!

Finish

Sticker the missing candy!

Add color.

Climb the marshmallow mountains!

Finish the mountains with sticker treats.

Jazzy juices!

Find the missing fruit stickers to create tasty drinks.

Delicious drinks!

35

Add extra fruit!

Sticker yummy food on the plate.

Hot-chocolate dip!

Follow the lines to see what gets dipped in the cup.

Pick-and-mix!

Sticker and trace the numbers to finish the sums.

three

◯ + **2** = **3**

four

2 + **2** =

eight

+ **5** = **8**

38

FILL the shelves of the candy shop

Color the fun
lollipops.

39

Use color and stickers to finish the shop's display.

fudge

Use the grids to help you draw the missing halves of the candy.

Baking buddies

The cookies are baking yummy treats.

Color bright toppings.

Oops! The cake has gone flat!

Find the missing stickers, then circle the one that is different.

Color the cute cookie cutters.

Pages 2–3

Pages 4–5

Pages 6–7

Pages 8–9

Pages 10–11

Pages 12–13

Pages 10–11 continued.

Pages 14–15

Pages 16–17

Pages 18–19

Pages 18-19 continued.

Pages 20-21

Pages 22-23

Pages 24-25

Pages 26-27

Pages 26–27 continued.

Pages 28–29

Pages 30–31

Pages 34–35

Pages 32–33

Pages 36–37

Extra stickers to use where you want.

Pages 36-37 continued.

Pages 38-40

3

4